HERBIE JONES

Sails into Second Grade

SUZY KLINE

HERBIE JONES

Sails into Second Grade

ILLUSTRATED BY **SAMI SWEETEN**

G. P. PUTNAM'S SONS

Special appreciation to . . .

Anne O'Connell, my editor for twenty years. Thank you for your love and dedication to the Herbie Jones characters. Thank you for being enthusiastic about this prequel.

Mrs. Donna Snyder and Mrs. Susan Goossen, who set sail each year with their second-grade sailors at Dudley Elementary in Fairport, New York. I still have the sailor's hat your class gave me. Happy retirement!

My dear friend Cindy Gelzinis and her second-graders at Southwest School in Torrington, Connecticut, who spelled all the ice cream flavors.

Mrs. Teresa Nakouzi at Beecher Road School in Woodbridge, Connecticut, for coming up with the "Herbie Jones and Ice Cream Cones" program.

The fifth-grade girls at Cherokee Bend Elementary School in Mountain Brook, Alabama, who gave Annabelle a yellow magic scarf. Thank you, Natalie Smith!

To Mr. Vance Teague, my fifth-grade teacher at Marin Elementary School in Albany, California, who always had us read our stories over a microphone. I loved writing in your class!

My funny husband, Rufus, who is a lot like Grandpa.

To my two loving daughters: Jennifer, who organized my school visits for four years, and Emily, who does it now.

And to Susan Kochan, my new editor, who thoughtfully helped me with this book.

—Suzy Kline

G. P. PUTNAM'S SONS
A division of Penguin Young Readers Group
Published by The Penguin Group
Penguin Group (USA) Inc., 375 Hudson Street, New York, NY 10014, U.S.A.
Penguin Group (Canada), 90 Eglinton Avenue East, Toronto, Ontario, Canada M4P 2Y3
(a division of Pearson Penguin Canada Inc.).
Penguin Books Ltd, 80 Strand, London WC2R 0RL, England.
Penguin Ireland, 25 St. Stephen's Green, Dublin 2, Ireland (a division of Penguin Books Ltd.).
Penguin Group (Australia), 250 Camberwell Road,
Camberwell, Victoria 3124, Australia (a division of Pearson Australia Group Pty Ltd).
Penguin Books India Pvt Ltd, 11 Community Centre, Panchsheel Park, New Delhi - 110 017, India.
Penguin Group (NZ), Cnr Airborne and Rosedale Roads,
Albany, Auckland 1310, New Zealand (a division of Pearson New Zealand Ltd).
Penguin Books (South Africa) (Pty) Ltd, 24 Sturdee Avenue, Rosebank,
Johannesburg 2196, South Africa.
Penguin Books Ltd, Registered Offices: 80 Strand, London WC2R 0RL, England.

Published simultaneously in Canada. Printed in the United States of America.
Design by Cecilia Yung and Marikka Tamura. Text set in 14-point Stone Informal.

Library of Congress Cataloging-in-Publication Data
Kline, Suzy. Herbie Jones sails into second grade / Suzy Kline ; illustrated by Sami Sweeten. p. cm.
Summary: Herbie meets a new teacher and makes a new friend on his first day of second grade.
[1. Schools—Fiction. 2. Friendship—Fiction.] I. Sweeten, Sami, ill. II. Title.
PZ7.K6797Hm 2006 [Fic]—dc22 2005003538
ISBN 0-399-22665-6
1 3 5 7 9 10 8 6 4 2
First Impression

Contents

Chapter One
Herbie's Secret Breakfast

"Herbie?" his mother called from the bathroom. "Please get your own breakfast this morning. I'm helping your sister with her hair."

"Okey-dokey," Herbie replied, rubbing his hands together. He liked doing things on his own.

Now, what could I get? Herbie thought as he walked into the kitchen.

Toast? Cereal? A banana? No. This was the first day of second grade. It should be something special. Something . . . secret!

"Herbie?" his mother called.

"Yes?"

"There are waffles in the freezer and fruit in the fridge."

"That's hunky-dory!" Herbie answered. His mom just gave him an idea.

Herbie got the first secret ingredient from the cupboard. He got the second secret ingredient from the freezer.

He was ready!

Herbie put two perfect scoops of Neapolitan ice cream into his waffle cone.

Ahhhhhhh, he thought as he licked his ice cream.

Mmmmmmm . . . creamy chocolate.

Ooooooooh . . . velvety vanilla.

"There's orange juice in the fridge," his mom called.

"Don't worry, Mom," Herbie replied. "I'll get some fruit." Then he bit into a strawberry that was half hidden in the ice cream.

Deeeeeeelicious!

Three minutes later, Herbie was crunching away at the cone. "Everything okay?" his mom shouted.

"It's the cat's pajamas!"

Mrs. Jones laughed. She liked it when Herbie used Grandpa's expressions.

One minute later, Olivia burst into the kitchen. "Don't eat all the corn . . . flakes."

Olivia froze. My brother is eating ice cream for *breakfast*? she thought. Olivia rolled her eyes, then bolted back down the hall.

Herbie knew he was doomed.

His special breakfast was no longer a secret.

Chapter Two
Off to School

Herbie wiped his mouth on a paper towel. He grabbed his new cowboy lunch box and stuffed it inside his old brown backpack.

Slowly he walked down the hallway. He knew he was doomed.

His sister and mom were standing by the full-length mirror.

"Dum da dum dum," he sang softly.

Herbie took a deep breath, then joined them.

"Hi, handsome," Mrs. Jones said. "You did a nice job combing your hair."

"Oh, Mom!" Olivia interrupted. "My first day in sixth grade has to be perfect! Is *my* hair okay? Is it too frizzy?"

Herbie raised his eyebrows. Olivia hadn't told! She was more interested in talking about her hair than tattling about his ice cream breakfast.

"I think your perm is lovely," his mother said.

Olivia was unsure. She was desperate for a second opinion. "Oh, I wish Daddy didn't have a night job," she moaned.

Suddenly she looked at
her brother. "What
do you think of
my new spiral
curls?"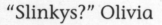

"They're just
like Slinkys."

"Slinkys?" Olivia
snapped. "Mom! Herbie's making fun of
my perm!"

Herbie shrugged. "Slinkys are cool!"

Brinnng! Brinnng!

"I'll get it!" Olivia yelled, dashing to the
kitchen.

Herbie raced his sister to the phone, but
she got there first.

"Hello . . . Oh, yes. We're on our way now. . . . No! We're not going to play hookey. We're going straight to school! . . . Yes! We have to leave right now. . . . Okay. I'll tell Herbie. . . . Love you too, Grandpa."

"What did he say?" Herbie asked, putting his finger in one of her Slinky curls.

Olivia took a step back. "He said to call him collect after school. He wants to hear about your first day."

"Hot dog!" Herbie exclaimed. His grandpa was special. He lived in California. Sometimes he came to Connecticut for a whole week visit.

After a long mommy hug, Herbie and Olivia hurried out the door.

As soon as they passed their yard, Herbie slowed down. "Thanks for not tattling on me."

"You're welcome," Olivia replied. "I needed Mom's help, and I was glad you didn't hog all the cornflakes. Now let's get going."

On the way to school, Herbie saw an
empty soda can on the sidewalk.

Herbie stepped on it.

He squished it.

He started kicking it.

"Do you have to do that?" Olivia asked.

Herbie didn't answer. He tapped the can with the side of his left sneaker.

Clink, clank.

"Okay, Herbie," Olivia groaned. "Just don't kick it at me."

Clink, clank.

"Hey, Herb. Did you know you're getting a new teacher? I hear Mrs. Schnellenberger was hired only last week!"

Olivia fired off a second question before Herbie could answer. "Who's that boy up the street? He's just standing there staring at you. Do you think he goes to our school?"

Herbie looked up. He had never seen

that boy before. He looked like a purple
crayon. He had on a purple top and purple
socks.

"If he does go to
our school, he isn't
in a hurry to get
there."

Chapter Three
The Purple Crayon

"Can I kick the can with you?" the new boy asked.

"Sure, have a turn," Herbie replied. "You new?"

"Yup, we just moved here last week from Minnesota. My favorite football team is the Vikings. My dad took me to a game once and got me this T-shirt."

"Cool," Herbie replied.

"So what's your name?" the boy asked.

"Herbie Jones. This is my sister, Olivia. What's yours?"

"Raymond Martin."

Herbie watched Raymond kick the can with the toe of his sneaker. It landed in the gutter.

"Ooops! Sorry! I always goof things up," Raymond said.

"No problem," Herbie replied. He picked up the can and dropped it on the sidewalk.

"You look like you're a second-grader too. Are you?" Olivia asked.

"Yup. I've got Mrs. Smelly Burger."

Herbie laughed.

"You mean Mrs. Schnellenberger?" Olivia corrected.

"Something like that," Raymond said.

Herbie kicked the can with the side of his sneaker. It rolled straight down the sidewalk.

Clink! Clank!

"Boy, you're good at kicking cans! Do you play soccer or something?" Raymond asked.

"No, but my uncle Dwight and I kick a can when we go on walks. Uncle Dwight goes to college at UConn, so he comes over a lot."

"Lucky you," Raymond replied. "That's my mom up there walking our new puppy. We just got him yesterday. He doesn't like the leash."

Herbie and Olivia looked at the little black dog. He was barking loudly as he ran circles around Raymond's mother. She was trying to untangle herself from the leash.

"What's your puppy's name?" Olivia asked.

"We don't have one yet."

Raymond took another turn kicking the can. This time he did it with the side of his sneaker.

Clink! Clank!

It landed in the middle of the sidewalk. Raymond jumped up and yelped like his dog.

Herbie clapped. "My uncle Dwight says if you can kick a can, you can do anything."

Olivia made a face.

"No kidding?" Raymond sighed. He wished that were true. Starting second grade was hard for him. He needed all the help he could get. Even help from a can.

"Hey!" Herbie said. "Your puppy is chasing your mom's shadow. That's why he's been running round and round."

"Shadow?" Raymond replied. "Shadow . . . That's a good name for him. Hey, SHADOW!" he yelled.

The dog stopped racing and looked back at Raymond.

He barked twice.

The boys laughed.

"He likes it!" Raymond said.

"He does!" Herbie agreed.

"So, what do you guys think your new teacher will be like?" Olivia asked.

"We'll find out soon," Herbie said. "We just need about ten more can kicks. Laurel Woods Elementary School is right around the corner."

Raymond made a face. He wished it were a million can kicks away.

Chapter Four
The Biggest Surprise!

When the boys got to their second-grade classroom, they saw rows of desks. Each one had a cardboard anchor hanging in front. Each anchor had a student's name. Herbie was glad his new friend Raymond sat nearby.

"Look at the boat books on the table!" Herbie said. "The one in the middle is about Viking ships."

Raymond was looking all around the room. He remembered sitting in the time-out chair in first grade. Now he wondered where he would sit when he got in trouble in second grade.

As soon as the bell rang, the girl sitting in front of Raymond started shushing everyone. "Shhh! Shhh! Shhh! I hear the

teacher's footsteps. She's coming down the hall right now."

Ka-thump, ka-thump, ka-thump.

Everyone sat up straight, folded their hands, and turned quiet.

Ka-thump, ka-thump, ka-thump.

The footsteps were really loud, Herbie thought.

The teacher finally stepped into the room.

Herbie's eyes bulged!

Ray's did too.

The teacher wasn't a she.

The teacher was a . . . he!

"Welcome, boys and girls, to second grade. I'm Mr. Schnellenberger, but you can call me Mr. S."

"He . . . he's a man!" Herbie blurted out.

"He's a giant!" John Greenweed said.

"He has big ears!" Phillip McDoogle whispered.

Mr. S smiled. "I'm six-foot-four, just like Abe Lincoln. I left my horse out back."

When no one laughed, the teacher

chuckled. "I'm kidding. I came to school on my bike."

"My uncle Dwight rides his bike to school too," Herbie whispered to Raymond.

Herbie got shushed again.

"Well, boys and girls," the teacher said. "It's anchors aweigh! I have something special in this big box for each one of you."

Herbie leaned forward, but he couldn't see what was inside.

Everyone watched Mr. S open up the flaps. Out came a pile of sailor hats. "We are going to sail through second grade together!"

Herbie beamed.

Each sailor hat had a name written on

it in Magic Marker. Mr. S held one up. The *shhh* girl came forward. Her sailor's hat said ANNABELLE in red.

Annabelle pulled it down on her head gently. She didn't want to smash her curls.

Herbie noticed she had a fuzzy yellow scarf wrapped around her neck. When she sat down, one end of it dropped on Ray's desk behind her.

The fuzzy scarf was shedding hairs like a dog. Ray picked up a few, then dropped the hairs to the floor like yellow parachutes.

"Look, Margie," Annabelle whispered. I got the first hat!" Margie had a long fuzzy scarf just like Annabelle's, only hers was pink.

Herbie rolled his eyes.

He didn't like braggers.

Or fuzz.

"John Greenweed," Mr. S called out.

John coughed. "Sometimes when I get

excited, I get an asthma attack," he said. "But I like being a sailor. Now I'm just like my uncle Bobby in the Navy!"

"All right!" the teacher replied. "Raymond Martin?"

Raymond took his hat. "Thanks, Mr. Burger."

The class laughed.

"Just call me Mr. S," the teacher said. "Hold the burger."

Raymond didn't laugh. He scooted down farther in his chair.

Herbie got the last hat. "It fits!" he said.

Mr. S saluted the class. "Everybody ready to set sail in second grade?"

"YES!" The kids saluted back.

Everyone except Raymond. He wasn't sure about going on any voyage.

"Okay," Mr. S replied. "Each morning, your sailor's hat will be on a hook, waiting for you. At the end of the day, you put it back!"

Herbie liked wearing a hat. He felt like he was really going somewhere.

Mr. S started singing:

"Sailing, sailing, over the ocean blue,

Sailing, sailing, away we go, Grade Two!"

The children joined him the second time he sang the song.

"Now, boys and girls," the teacher said, "it is time to do some writing. I want to know what you like to do. Write a few sentences in the notebook on your desk. You each have a sharpened pencil. So please begin."

Herbie started to think.

What did he like to do? When Raymond's

stomach growled, Herbie knew.

Chapter Five
The Magic Scarf

Herbie pulled his sailor's hat down over his forehead and smiled. Writing a few sentences was easy! He felt like he was sailing through second grade.

I love to eat ice creem cones. Espeshly vennla, chocklet, stroobery, oring sherbert, chocklet chip, roke rode, peperment sick and neopeltin. I had a neopeltin ice creem today. It was the best brekfast I ever had.

Annabelle tapped Herbie on the shoulder. "I like the horse on your sweater. You didn't spell all your words correctly."

Herbie made a face. Who was this girl? She could say something nice and mean at the same time.

"Okay, class," the teacher said. "I want you to read aloud what you wrote. I'm passing this little plastic tape recorder from desk to desk. It has a microphone. Please use it. That way we'll hear every word!"

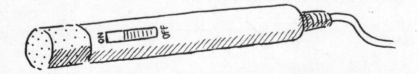

Herbie gazed back at Raymond. He was fiddling with Annabelle's fuzzy scarf.

Annabelle raised her hand politely.

"May I go first, Mr. S?"

"Yes!"

Herbie noticed Annabelle had her own pencils. Each one had her name engraved in gold. She also had a brand-new leather book bag. It wasn't beat-up like his.

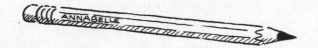

Annabelle took the tape recorder and pressed the ON button. "Testing . . . testing. I've done this before." She cleared her throat.

"If you hold the microphone too close, it makes a shrill noise," Annabelle said. "I know."

Herbie and Raymond exchanged a look. Annabelle was a know-it-all, they thought.

Annabelle began reading. "I love wearing my magic scarf. It's a new fad in Laurel Woods. Mine is bright yellow. It's fuzzy, very long, very soft, and it's hollow. It's magic because you can even pull it over your head

and wear it like a dress. I wear it like an accent scarf. It matches the yellow daisies on the pockets of my pants."

Annabelle turned the page. She had written two full pages. While she read aloud, Raymond put his hand inside the tail end of her hollow scarf.

"I also love ballet, playing soccer, petting my Siamese cat, Sukey, and drawing daisies. I read the most books at our Laurel Woods Library this summer. I got a blue ribbon for reading over one hundred books."

Suddenly, the class broke out laughing. Annabelle quickly looked around. There was Raymond, wearing a hat. Not a sailor's

hat like everyone else, but the tail end of her yellow fuzzy scarf.

Annabelle flared her nostrils.

Mr. S. smiled. "We can see that Raymond was listening. He's testing out Annabelle's magic scarf right now!"

Raymond half smiled. Mr. S was the first teacher he ever had who didn't yell at him for doing something silly.

Herbie thought Ray looked like a yellow Santa Claus with all that fuzz around his face. When Raymond yanked the scarf off his head, his hair stuck out all over. Now the class laughed for a second time.

Annabelle immediately yanked her magic scarf away. She made sure both ends were on her lap.

"Very good," Mr. S said. "I always like hairy adventures. Who would like to go next?"

John did after he added a long sentence. "I'm an Eel in the YMCA swim program. I go every Saturday morning with my dad. I love to jump off the high dive. I love making a big splash. I can do a real good cannonball. I like to read about sea turtles. I got a red ribbon for reading the second most books at our Laurel Woods Library this summer."

"What wonderful writers and readers I

have!" the teacher said. "Raymond, would you share yours next?"

Raymond put the microphone next to his lips. "I love . . ."

The recorder made a shrill noise.

Everyone covered their ears.

Annabelle whispered to Margie, "Look at Raymond's sloppy work. He scribbles."

Raymond's heart began beating faster. He heard Annabelle's mean words.

She knew.

Soon everyone else would too.

School was hard for Raymond.

"So what?" Margie whispered to Annabelle. "Raymond knows what he wrote."

When Margie gave Raymond a warm smile, he felt better. Raymond held the microphone farther away. "I love going to Burger Paradise. I love cheeseburgers. I love french fries. I love Bits O'Chicken. I love milk shakes. I love Paradise pickles. I wish my teacher's name was Mr. Hamburger."

All the kids laughed.

Raymond peeked at Mr. S. He was
smiling.

"Good ending!" Mr. S said. "You're a
writer, Ray!"

A writer? Raymond looked surprised.
No one had ever told him that before.

Herbie's turn was next. He read all four sentences over the microphone. When he finished, everyone clapped.

"Herbie Jones likes ice cream cones," the teacher said.

"Hey, that rhymes!" John exclaimed.

"It does!" Mr. S agreed. "I think Herbie and Ray have a lot in common. They both like to write about food!"

Raymond flashed a toothy smile.

Suddenly, he felt hopeful. Maybe that fuzzy scarf *was* magic. He had touched it enough.

"I can sail through second grade if Herbie sails with me," he said bravely. Then Raymond put his sailor's hat on his head.

Mr. S gave Ray the thumbs-up sign.

Herbie gave Ray two thumbs up. He liked

his new friend.

Chapter Six
Candy for Breakfast?

erbie waited for the fourth ring.

"Howdy-howdy-howdy," the voice said at the other end.

The operator replied immediately. "Will you accept a phone call from Herbie Jones?"

"Okey-dokey!"

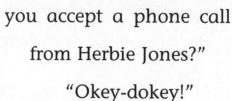

"GRANDPA, I'M SAILING IN SECOND GRADE! We get to wear sailor hats in class!"

"That's hunky-dory!" Grandpa replied.

"Yeah," Herbie agreed. "It's the cat's pajamas."

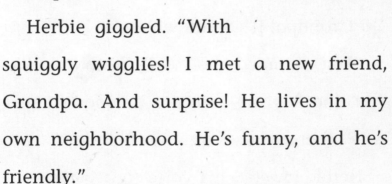

"With polka dots or stripes?"

Herbie giggled. "With squiggly wigglies! I met a new friend, Grandpa. And surprise! He lives in my own neighborhood. He's funny, and he's friendly."

"Well, tickle the bees and climb trees!" Grandpa replied. "What's his name?"

"Ray. He likes cheeseburgers and I like ice cream cones. We wrote about it in class. He also has a dog, and I helped name him."

"Fido?"

"No." Herbie giggled.

"Spot?"

"Noooooo!" Herbie loved his guessing games with his grandpa.

"Pickles?"

"Grandpa! It's Shadow!"

"You stumped me! Well, it sounds like you and Ray are going to be good friends. Any other surprises on your first day?"

Herbie lowered his voice to a whisper. "I had ice cream for breakfast, and Olivia didn't tattle."

"All righty!" Grandpa replied. "Did you have candy too? That's what I have for breakfast."

"Nooooo," Herbie snapped. "You don't eat candy for breakfast."

"You're right. I eat it for dinner."

"Grandpa!"

Grandpa giggled, then he got serious. "Well, nobody has a perfect day. Anything turn out to be a dud?"

"Yeah, I sit next to a girl named Annabelle and I don't like her."

"That's what I said once about your grandma."

"No kidding?" Herbie replied.

"No kidding," Grandpa said.

"Well, I gotta go, Grandpa. I don't want you to have a big phone bill. I love you."

"I love you too. See you soon, big baboon."

"Bye-bye, hairy fly!" Herbie replied.

When Herbie hung up, he realized he left out the biggest surprise about his first day in second grade.

Oh well, he thought, I'll tell Grandpa about Mr. S next time.